DETROIT PUBLIC LIBRARY

D1488960

Scary Stories for Campfires

Parkman Branch Library
1766 Oakman Blvd.
Detroit, MI 48238

Sterling Publishing Co., Inc.
New York

Library of Congress Cataloging-in-Publication Data Available

10 9 8 7 6 5 4 3 2 1

Published by Sterling Publishing Co., Inc.
387 Park Avenue South, New York, NY 10016
© 2005 by Sterling Publishing Co., Inc.
Material in this book originally published in *World's Best True Ghost
Stories* by C.B. Colby, © 1990 by Sterling Publishing Co., Inc.; *World's
Best Lost Treasure Stories*, © 1991 by C.B. Colby; *World's Strangest True
Ghost Stories* by John Macklin, © 1991 by Sterling Publishing Co., Inc.;
World's Most Mystifying True Ghost Stories, © 1997 by Ron Edwards;
Scary Howl Of Fame, by Sheryl Scarborough and Sharon McCoy, ©
1995 by RGA Publishing Group, Inc.; *World's Most Bone-Chilling
"True" Ghost Stories*, © 1993 by Sterling Publishing Co., Inc.; *World's
Most Terrifying "True" Ghost Stories*, © 1995 by Arthur Myers, and
World's Scariest "True" Ghost Stories, © 1994 by Margaret Rau.
Distributed in Canada by Sterling Publishing
c/o Canadian Manda Group, 165 Dufferin Street
Toronto, Ontario, Canada M6K 3H6
Distributed in Great Britain and Europe by Chris Lloyd at Orca Book
Services, Stanley House, Fleets Lane, Poole BH15 3AJ, England
Distributed in Australia by Capricorn Link (Australia) Pty. Ltd.
P.O. Box 704, Windsor, NSW 2756, Australia

Printed in China
All rights reserved

Sterling ISBN 1-4027-2170-6

For information about custom editions, special sales, premium and
corporate purchases, please contact Sterling Special Sales
Department at 800-805-5489 or specialsales@sterlingpub.com.

CONTENTS

1

Haunted Habitats   5

The Evil in Room 310   6
The Haunted Schoolhouse   8
The Doctor's Visitor   9
The Ghost of Dead Man's Curve   11
The Light in the Window   13

2

Entertaining Ghosts   15

Lucky at Cards   16
Sam Plays the Ghost from South Troy   18
The Weekend Guest Who Wasn't There   20

3

Famous Phantoms   23

Not Gone with the Wind   24
The Beautiful Blonde of Brentwood   25
Washington Irving Returns   27
Valentino's Ring   28

4

Ghostly Animals   31

The Case of the Kitten Ghost   32
A Horse Named Lady Wonder   35
Ghost Dog on the Stairway   39

5

What's in the House?   41

The Thing in the Cellar   42
The Headless Lady   44
The Ghost of Greylock   46
The Haunted Cleaning Lady   48
The Demonic Hairdresser   51

6

Ghouls on the Move   53
The Phantom Stagecoach   54
The Runaway Locomotive   56
Faces in the Sea   59

7

Messages from Beyond   61
The Ghost of a Deformed Monk   62
A Terrifying Visitor   63
Deadly Kindness   64
A Lady's Reign of Death   67

8

Tales of Terror   69
The Terrible Hand   70
What Got Oliver Latch?   72
The Boy with the Brass Buttons   74

9

Stranger Than Fiction   77
The Old Man of the Woods   78
The Hunter and the Hunted   80
The Man and the Glove   83
The Spell on the Mirror   85

10

Spirited Encounters   87
Death at the Falls   88
The Fourth Presence   91
Lavender   94

Index   96

1

Haunted Habitats

The Evil in Room 310

Marsha Bennett told me this story herself. She had been north to visit friends in the state of Washington. Now she was driving back to her home in California. The last lap of the day's journey was over the Cascade Range that stretches from Washington to California. It was late evening and snow had begun to fall before she finally reached the little Oregon town where she planned to spend the night.

Tired and ready for a hot meal and a good night's sleep, she stopped at the first place she came upon. It was an old hotel on the main street. The lobby had a musty odor. The seedy clerk behind the desk signed her in. Her room was on the third floor—Room 310. An elderly bellhop helped her with her luggage.

As soon as the door was opened, a blast of hot air struck Marsha full in the face. With the hot air came something else, something she could not define but that filled her with dread. It was heavy and depressing, she explained, "with the strong scent of evil." She felt as if she was about to faint.

All she said was, "It's awfully hot."

The bellhop tinkered with the radiator knobs. Then he opened the window and left. The room began to cool off, but the feeling of despair and dread grew stronger. It centered on the open square of black window space. The terror seemed to speak in her mind. "Go to the window," it said. "Throw yourself out, out, out!" Terrified, Marsha flung herself on the bed farthest from the window.

"I kept saying no, no, no to that voice," she told me, "but the voice kept insisting."

"You can't fight me, you puny thing," it said. "Sooner or later you'll jump. I'll make you! Jump! Jump! Jump!"

At last Marsha could stand it no longer. She jumped up, calling herself a coward. "Coward or not," she explained, "I was sure that if I stayed the night, I'd be dead by morning."

Marsha was prepared to sacrifice the money she'd already paid just to leave, but when she went downstairs with her baggage to check out, the clerk never asked what was wrong or if she wished to try another room. He returned the full cash amount to her.

Marsha drove down the street to a modern motel. As she entered the lobby, she felt the dark depression slip from her shoulders. She became almost giddy with relief. She had planned to be on her way early the next morning. Instead she decided to stay over a day and look into the history of the old hotel to see if she could discover the reason for her terrifying experience there.

She visited the local library to make a few inquiries. An elderly librarian sat behind the desk.

"I'm just wondering," Marsha said tentatively. "Did anything shocking ever happen in the old hotel?"

The librarian looked at her strangely. "How did you come upon that bit of history?" she asked. "It took the hotel a long time to squash the story."

The librarian went on to tell what had happened. One evening back in 1948 a couple checked into the hotel as Mr. and Mrs. Oscar Smith. The next morning hotel employees found the young woman's body lying on the sidewalk outside the hotel beneath Room 310. The man who had registered as her husband had disappeared.

"At first it was ruled suicide," the librarian concluded. "But then they pried open her fist and found it clutched a handful of dark curly hair, not her own. So they made a search for the murderer. But he was never found . . .

"By the way," the librarian suddenly added, "isn't that a coincidence! It all happened on November 5, forty years ago yesterday."

The Haunted Schoolhouse

The small schoolhouse in Newburyport, Massachusetts, was the scene of a strange phenomenon in 1870. Every day a mysterious yellow glow spread over the classroom, windows, and blackboards. It usually started near the hall door and spread silently over the room. After about two minutes it faded away. It did no harm while it cast its light over the room, but afterward the students and their teacher, Miss Lucy A. Perkins, felt weak and ill.

The yellow radiance was not the only unusual occurrence. It was accompanied by a gust of cold air that swept through the room, even when the doors and windows were tightly closed. The chill breeze rustled the papers, swung the faded map on the wall, and shook the hanging oil lamp. This too, made the teacher and children feel slightly ill, but Miss Perkins kept the class going day after day, bravely trying to ignore the strange event.

In the late fall, the yellow light disappeared and a low-pitched laugh was heard. The eerie sound echoed in the school's tiny attic, the small coal cellar, and the hall. One day, many of the students, along with Miss Perkins, saw a child's hand floating in the air. Then the arm became visible.

The climax came on November 1. During a geography lesson, Miss Perkins called upon a student to recite. In the midst of a sentence he suddenly stopped and pointed to the hall. There stood a boy with his arm upraised. It was the same arm and hand that had floated in the air.

The mysterious boy stood silently, his face bound in a white cloth as though he had an injured jaw or a toothache. Then, as they watched, he slowly vanished. From that time on, the schoolhouse was plagued no more.

In an attempt to solve the mystery, the authorities questioned three local boys who had a reputation for mischief, but they decided the trio had no part in the events. To this day, the yellow glow, the cold breeze, and the boy with the upraised arm and bandaged jaw have never been explained.

The Doctor's Visitor

Dr. S. Weir Mitchell of Philadelphia was one of the nation's foremost neurologists during the latter part of the 19th century. One snowy evening after a particularly hard day, he retired early, and was just falling asleep when his doorbell rang loudly. He hoped it had been a trick of his hearing, or that his caller would go away, but the bell rang again even more insistently. Struggling awake, he snatched a robe and stumbled down to see who it was. He muttered in annoyance as he slid the bolt to unlock the door, completely unprepared for the shivering child who stood in the swirling snow.

The small, pale girl trembled on the doorstep, for a thin frock and a ragged shawl were her only protection against the blustering snow-filled wind. She said in a tiny, plaintive voice, "My mother is very sick—won't you come, please?"

Dr. Mitchell explained that he had retired for the night and suggested that the child call another doctor in the vicinity. But she wouldn't leave, and looking up at him with tear-filled eyes,

pleaded again, "Won't *you* come, please?" No one—and certainly no doctor—could refuse this pitiful appeal.

With a resigned sigh, thinking longingly of his warm bed, the physician asked the child to step inside while he dressed and picked up his bag. Then he followed her into the storm. In a house several streets away he found a woman desperately sick with pneumonia. He recognized her immediately as someone who had once worked for him as a servant, and he bent over the bed, determined to save her. As he worked, the doctor complimented her on her daughter's fortitude and persistence in getting him there.

The woman stared at the doctor in disbelief and said in a weak whisper, "That cannot be. My little girl died more than a month ago. Her dress is still hanging in that cupboard over there!"

With strange emotions, Dr. Mitchell strode to the cupboard and pulled open the door. Inside hung the little dress and the tattered shawl that his caller had worn. They were warm and dry and could never have been out in the storm!

The Ghost of Dead Man's Curve

In 1908, a trolley line in New York State ran from Port Chester to Rye Village and Rye Beach. The tracks crossed one road that was really just a right-of-way raised up over a swamp. A hand-operated switch at the crossing point could throw the trolley on either of two routes.

This swampland was full of tall reeds, cattails, pools of dark evil-smelling water, and, reputedly, quicksand—a highly unlikely place for human beings to venture. But apparently one unfortunate person did. Or did he?

Late one night the trolley rocked and clattered down the tracks to the crossing point. The motorman stopped and got down to throw the switch so that he could proceed toward Rye. There were two passengers in the huge, dimly lit car, one man seated at each end. Neither man paid any particular attention to the other.

After the motorman had climbed down to the switch, one of the passengers also got up and left the car. The switch was thrown. The motorman came back to his post, and the car started along, picking up speed.

For some time the remaining passenger did not realize that the other man had not returned. When he did, and told the motorman, the trolley was almost in Rye.

The motorman reported the lost traveler, and a search party was quickly organized, for the swamp was known to be treacherous. But neither that search party nor one formed the next day could find any trace of the missing man. Where could he have gone?

The most logical explanation was that the man, probably a stranger, had set off across the swamp and perished in one of the bottomless pools, or in quicksand. Nothing, certainly, was ever seen or heard of him again.

From then on, until the trolley line was discontinued, that crossing point in the swamp was known as "Dead Man's Curve," and people gave it a wide berth on dark nights or gloomy days. Those who did occasionally walk along the tracks often reported low moans, faint calls for help, whistling, and splashing from deep in the marshland.

Perhaps they were the natural voices of the swamp, the calls of birds, or the moaning of wind in the bulrushes...or perhaps they were the regretful cries of the shade of an ill-fated traveler, who stepped out of a trolley and into eternity.

The Light in the Window

O n a train traveling west through Canada one night, some of us were sitting up pretty late telling yarns. One fellow told this story.

A friend of his who lived in Ontario once became fascinated with an old painting he saw in a dingy little store. It showed a dramatic-looking castle on a hilltop. The scene was dark, mysterious and gloomy. Every window in the castle was dark—except for a small, arched casement high in a stone tower. The man wondered why anyone would paint a castle with a light in just one window. Was there a story behind it?

He bought the painting and hung it in his home, but all the storekeeper could tell him was that it depicted a castle in Scotland. There was neither signature nor date.

One day, as he was cleaning the painting, he found a few Latin words in a corner. He asked a friend to translate the

words, and learned that they meant "every century it will be dark." This inscription made little sense to him, and he forgot about it.

The painting hung in the man's home for many years. Sitting around after dinner, he and his friends enjoyed speculating about who was in the tower and why the window was lighted. It was quite a conversation piece.

One evening the owner of the painting was telling some guests about how he had acquired it, and answered questions about its background and meaning. The guests wanted to see this unusual and mysterious piece of art, so they all trooped into the hall where it hung.

Imagine their astonishment and the consternation of their host when they saw that, on the painting, the window in the tower was dark! Examining the painting closely, they were astounded to see that the black paint on the once light-yellow window was as old and cracked as the paint on the rest of the picture. There were no signs that it had ever been different, let alone bright yellow.

After the guests had gone, the embarrassed host unsuccessfully tried to find a solution to the puzzle. The next morning he returned to the painting and felt his skin crawl. The window in the tower was lighted! Then he thought of the Latin inscription, "Every century it will be dark." He made a note of the date and began a serious search into Scottish history.

Eventually these facts were uncovered: The castle had been the home of an evil character who had two sons. He hated the elder son and kept him locked in the tower, while his younger son enjoyed all the wealth and pleasures his father could give him.

Exactly five hundred years before the night when the painted window had gone dark, the imprisoned elder son had died in the little room high in the tower.

2
Entertaining Ghosts

Lucky at Cards

It was a cold and stormy night in the late 1890s. The patrons of the Buxton Inn in Maine were sitting around a roaring fire in the taproom, swapping yarns. Suddenly, a young man entered. His rich clothes were trimmed with gold lace and he carried a cape over his arm. He shook the snow from his tall beaver hat, stamped his booted feet, and strode to the fireplace.

The others looked up with interest, admiring his elegance, but also noting that his clothes were old-fashioned and a bit strange. Undoubtedly, they thought, he was a traveler from some distant city. One of them offered him a place close to the fire, and suggested that he join them in a game of cards. With a cheerful smile he agreed.

As the evening and the game progressed, the young man had uncanny good luck in every deal of the cards. The other players all felt that there was something familiar about the handsome young man, as though they had seen him many times before but couldn't place him. Oddly enough, he knew many of them by name, but never introduced himself.

It was nearly morning when another patron entered. As he removed his coat and boots, he called to the innkeeper. "What's happened to your sign? I thought I had the wrong tavern."

The others, surprised, looked out the window to see the swinging sign outside the door. Wiping the steam from the glass, they saw with astonishment that there was nothing upon the sign but the words "Buxton Inn." The painting of a young cavalier was gone. Then they knew.

With wonder and fright they turned back to the fireplace, but the dapper young card player was gone, leaving nothing but a small puddle of melted snow beneath the chair where his boots had rested. No wonder he had looked familiar.

Almost fearfully they turned again to look at the tavern's sign. Was it a trick of the storm? For now, as clearly as ever, they could see the painting of young Sir Charles in his tall beaver hat and flowing cape, as he had stood for many years. Then something else caught their eye—something they had never noticed before. One of the pockets of his breeches seemed to be bulging as though with many coins, and a smile played about the painted mouth—the kind of smile a young man might wear when he has been lucky at cards.

Sam Plays the Ghost
from South Troy

Aghost in South Troy, New York, was a kindly soul who paid dividends in dollars for decent behavior toward him. His story has been circulating for many years now, and while no one seems to know what happened to the people involved, it goes like this.

Although the old house in South Troy was quite well furnished, it was never occupied for long. The tenants always found some excuse for moving out after a few weeks or even days. They said it was too scary to live in, and all gave the same account as to why.

It seems that every midnight a white-bearded old man, tall and thin, came clumping down from the attic and stalked into the parlor, where he stopped in front of some oil paintings and tapped them with his cane or pointed at them. After this he would clump out again and up to his attic. No one could touch him or stop him, but everyone could see him. It was said that if you stood in front of him he would walk right through you and it felt like a cool breeze blowing in your face. He'd never stop, even if the doors were locked shut before him.

Many tenants, as might be expected, told their stories to Sam, the saloonkeeper at Jefferson and First Streets. Sam never blinked. The landlord was beginning to think he would never rent the place to anyone, when he hit on an idea. He offered Sam and two friends of his a hundred dollars each to spend the night there. Sam, the landlord thought, would see no ghost and would soon dispel the fear in South Troy. Sam agreed and took his friends to the house to play pinochle.

But at the stroke of midnight, the old man did clump down again, and Sam saw him, just as he had been described. Without a word he went to the oil paintings, tapped each with his cane, and then started back up toward the attic. Sam stood in his way and got walked through, but it didn't perturb him. It seemed to Sam that the old man was rather lonely and unhappy if he went about walking through people without saying hello.

Sam ran around to the front of the old man and gestured toward the pinochle table, offering him a chance to sit in on a few hands. The old man frowned, puzzled, for a few moments. Then he floated over to the table and sat down. He couldn't hold the cards too well, due possibly to fluctuations in his ectoplasm. Occasionally his fingers would become transparent and the cards would fall to the table. He would seem to apologize. Also, Sam reported, he played a rather naïve game of pinochle. Sam debated whether to throw the game to make the old man happy, but he decided against it.

After a half-hour of pinochle the old man was apparently bored. He rose, banged heavily on the oil paintings with his cane—one, two, ten times—and clumped back up to the attic, nodding politely to Sam, but yawning nevertheless.

After some thought, Sam went to the paintings and took them down. The wallpaper behind them had a fist-size hollow with no plaster behind it. Sam stuck his hand through the paper and pulled out over $50,000 in United States Government Series E War Bonds. He later used them to open a large cocktail lounge on Second and Washington Streets.

The old man continued to be seen, however. It is said he clumps down from the attic even today. His entire hoard is gone and he carries no cane or pointer, merely a mournful expression on his face, as if he feels he may have paid too much for a half-hour's entertainment!

The Weekend Guest
Who Wasn't There

It was on a June morning in 1936 that Dr. John Rowley, a general practitioner in a rural district in England's West Country, received a letter that led to the strangest episode of his life. The letter came from Arthur Sherwood, a former medical-school colleague now practicing in London.

"Thank you for your invitation for a long weekend," he wrote. "A spell in the country would doubtless do me a world of good. I will travel by the 10:30 train on Friday."

So it was that Dr. Rowley became involved in one of the most curious and inexplicable stories of the century.

On the day of his friend's arrival, Dr. Rowley had an early lunch and set off for Exeter to meet the London train. Passing a bus stop in his car, he noticed a friend who was an architect, and stopped to give him a lift. As the station was some distance from the center of town, the doctor invited his friend to meet the train with him. Afterward, he would make a small detour and drop his friend off at his office.

The architect agreed. They arrived at the station five minutes before the train was due and parked the car. Then they walked up to the bridge that spanned the tracks and leaned over it, so they had a complete view of the platform at which the train would arrive.

The train was three minutes early, and only four passengers debarked—three men and a young woman. One of the men was Dr. Sherwood. "That's him," Dr. Rowley said, pointing to a thickset man in a raincoat and bowler hat.

Dr. Rowley shouted down a greeting. The man looked up, waved, and smiled; then, picking up his suitcase, he hurried out of sight toward the station exit.

Rowley and his companion walked down to meet him. The

other men and the girl came out, but there was no sign of Dr. Sherwood.

"Did the man in the bowler hat already go through?" Dr. Rowley asked the ticket collector.

"Only three people got off the train," he replied. "And they have come through." He held out, as proof, three tickets.

Both the doctor and the architect protested that there was a mistake. They were allowed through the barrier and searched the station buildings for over half an hour, but found no one.

Disturbed and bewildered, Dr. Rowley returned home. He had been in the house just a few minutes when a telegram arrived.

It was from Dr. Sherwood's partner in London—and it reported that Dr. Sherwood had been fatally injured that morning in a street accident soon after leaving home for his weekend in the country.

A telephone call confirmed this was true. Dr. Sherwood had been knocked down by a taxi and taken, unconscious, to a hospital, where he died as the result of a fractured skull.

What possible explanation could there be? Later, at the request of Dr. Rowley, Francis Grafton, the architect who had accompanied him to the station, wrote the following statement:

"It was nearly 10:30 a.m. when I accompanied the doctor to the railway station. The sun was out and the light extremely good. We were standing on the bridge waiting for the train, barely fifty yards from the platform.

"Four passengers definitely alighted from the train—three men and a young woman. Of this, I am quite sure. The eldest passenger was a man in a raincoat and bowler hat and carrying a case. Dr. Rowley pointed him out to me as the man he had come to meet. When Dr. Rowley hailed him, the passenger smiled and waved.

"When we got to the barrier, only three people were waiting to come through. I am of a skeptical nature, and do not believe in ghosts. Nevertheless, I am completely unable to give any rational explanation of the incident. I confess it is an utter mystery to me."

Is there an explanation?

Psychic researchers call this type of ghost a "subjective" phantom. They suggest that it is a hybrid being, created by the disembodied spirit of the dead person combining with some "piece of matter" to produce a temporary, though very elementary, intelligence.

Other authorities insist that this sort of ghost is a timeless "thought-form" produced by people of the past, present, and future—an image of another world that becomes perceptible to certain people under special conditions. This, say the experts, was probably what was seen by the men on the bridge—the image of a man who had slipped temporarily into another dimension of time and space.

You may not agree with this explanation. But can you think of any other

3

Famous Phantoms

Not Gone with the Wind

One magnificent mansion in Atlanta is among the few antebellum homes to escape the disastrous fire during the Civil War. It was unharmed by General William Sherman as he marched through Georgia in 1864. The stately house was built on three-hundred acres of woodland five years before the first shot was fired at Fort Sumter in April 1861.

Many ghosts have dropped in on this house, but the most famous visitor is the author whose epic novel about the Old South became a classic motion picture in 1939. The spirit of Margaret Mitchell first appeared in the spring, several years after she sold the house. She had intended to help the new owner restore the antique mansion but died in 1946, when she was hit by a car.

Margaret Mitchell had wanted to preserve the elegant estate that served as a model for Tara in her novel, *Gone with the Wind*. On her first ethereal visit "she came through the closed door," said the owner. "Now she comes every year, carrying flowers and wearing a green dress. She never speaks. Instead, she always has an armful of jonquils as she wanders through the house."

After the first time the owner saw the famous author's ghost, he went to visit her grave. Her plot was covered by a bed of jonquils. Perhaps she wants to remain in the house that in life was so dear to her heart.

The Beautiful Blonde of Brentwood

Once upon a time, a lonely teenage girl named Norma Jean Baker left her foster home and became a model. A few years later, she was earning seventy-five dollars a week as a contract player at 20th Century Fox. Norma Jean would soon become Marilyn Monroe and eventually a screen legend in her own time, as a beautiful Hollywood movie queen.

On August 5, 1962, the world was stunned to hear that the blonde goddess had died in her home on Helena Drive in Brentwood, a suburb of Los Angeles, California.

Marilyn Monroe had a lifetime interest in the supernatural. She often consulted astrologers and psychics for reassurance and comfort during frequent periods of depression and unhappiness.

One morning around 12:15, a couple was driving through Marilyn's former neighborhood on their way home. As they passed the star's last home, they slowed down when a blonde woman, wearing white slacks and loafers, suddenly appeared on the lawn. When the apparition came closer, the curious pair recognized the woman as Marilyn Monroe. She continued walking toward the car, and then disappeared.

Some have seen Marilyn make her way across the lawn, then move near a tree and clasp her hands. Others have seen her glide from the house and into the street before fading away.

Unlike most dwellings of the rich and famous in Beverly Hills, the enigmatic star's house was not a grand mansion on a landscaped lawn. The modest, single-story home featured small rooms and privacy. A coat-of-arms adornment placed near the front door announced, *Cursum Perficio*, which means "I am finishing my journey." The proverb came true.

Marilyn Monroe loved her Mexican-style house—the only home she owned during her life—and it may be the reason she came back to visit, after her death.

Washington Irving Returns

Libraries are wonderful storerooms for books offering adventure, romance, and mystery. The Astor Library in New York also offers a famous ghost.

In 1860, Dr. J.G. Cogswell was working there late one evening when he heard a sound a few aisles away. He got up, walked around a bookcase, and saw an old man reading at a table.

The stranger looked familiar, but Cogswell could not identify him in the sparse lighting. As he approached the shadowy figure, he realized he was looking at his old friend, Washington Irving, who had written over a dozen literary classics.

There was only one thing wrong. Washington Irving had been dead for several months, and Cogswell had been a pallbearer at Irving's funeral!

As Cogswell began walking toward his friend, the ghostly figure vanished.

A few nights later, Cogswell was again working alone in the library when he saw his dead friend hunched over a book. The glowing, white-haired phantom seemed oblivious to Cogswell and disappeared before the doctor could speak.

Cogswell finally told his friends about the supernatural visit and was advised to spend a few days relaxing in the country.

But he was not the only person to see the famous author. Pierre Irving, the writer's nephew, saw his uncle at the family residence in Tarrytown, New York. The apparition appeared in the parlor and walked to the room where Washington Irving created *Rip Van Winkle* and other masterpieces.

Pierre stared quietly at his uncle's spirit. He was as shocked as Ichabod Crane meeting the Headless Horseman. Moments later, the hazy image faded away.

Ironically, the author of *The Legend of Sleepy Hollow*—America's first ghost story—did not believe in the supernatural. He would probably be amused to learn that he would become the most celebrated ghost in New York.

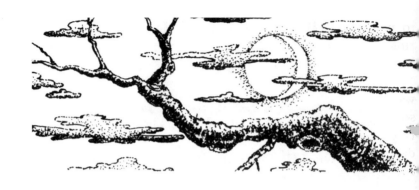

Valentino's Ring

I n the vault of a Los Angeles bank lies a silver ring set with a semiprecious stone. It is not a particularly pretty ring or even a very valuable one, and chances are that no one will ever dare to wear it again. It lies in the vault because it bears one of the most malignant curses in the history of the occult. Successive owners have suffered injury, misfortune, even death.

And many people still believe it was this ring that sent Rudolph Valentino to a premature grave. Certainly, the violent incidents that have surrounded it over the years can hardly be shrugged off as mere coincidences.

It was in 1920 that Valentino, at the peak of his success, saw the ring in a San Francisco jeweler's. The proprietor warned him that the ring was a jinx, but Valentino still bought it.

He wore the ring in his next picture, *The Young Rajah*. It was the biggest flop of his career and he was off the screen for the next two years.

Valentino did not wear the ring again until he used it as a costume prop in *The Son of the Sheik*. Three weeks after finishing this film, he went to New York on vacation. While wearing the ring, he suffered an acute attack of appendicitis. Two weeks later, he was dead.

Pola Negri, a famous female movie star of the time, asked

to pick a memento from Valentino's possessions, chose the ring—and almost immediately suffered a long period of ill health that threatened to end her career.

A year later, while convalescing, she met a performer who was almost Valentino's double, Russ Colombo. Miss Negri was so struck by the resemblance that she gave him Rudolph's ring, saying, "From one Valentino to another." Within a few days of receiving the gift, Russ Colombo was killed in a freak shooting accident.

His cousin passed the ring on to Russ's best friend, Joe Casino. Also at the height of his popularity as an entertainer, Casino took no chances with the ring. Instead of wearing it, he kept it in a glass case in memory of his dead friend. When he was asked to donate it to a museum of Valentino relics, he refused, saying that he treasured it for sentimental reasons.

As time passed, Joe Casino forgot the ring's evil reputation and put it on. A week later, still wearing the ring, he was knocked down by a truck and killed.

By now the curse was front-page news. When asked what he proposed to do with the ring, Joe's brother, Del, explained that he could not allow himself to be intimidated by a curse, or jinx, or ghost, or whatever it was. He didn't believe in things like that. Del Casino wore the ring for some time and nothing unusual happened. Then he lent it to a collector of Valentino relics, who suffered no ill effects either. This caused several newspapers to speculate that at last the evil influence of the ring had come to an end. And that seemed to trigger off a new wave of violence.

One night soon afterward, the home of Del Casino was burgled. The police saw the burglar, a man named James Willis, running from the scene. One of them fired a warning shot, but the bullet went low and killed Willis. Among the loot found in his possession was the Valentino ring.

It was at this time that Hollywood producer Edward Small decided to make a film based on Valentino's career.

Jack Dunn, a former skating partner to ice star Sonja Henie, bore a great resemblance to Rudolph and was asked to make a film test for the part. He dressed in Valentino's clothes for the test—and also wore the jinxed ring. Only twenty-one years old at the time, Dunn died ten days later from a rare blood disease.

After this tragedy the ring was kept out of sight and never worn by anyone again, but that did not seem to curb its fatal influence.

A year after Jack Dunn's death, a daring raid was carried out in broad daylight on a Los Angeles bank in which thieves got away with a haul of over $200,000. In a subsequent police ambush, two of the gang were caught and three passersby seriously injured. The leader of the bank robbers, Alfred Hahn, was jailed for life.

At his trial, Hahn remarked: "If I'd known what was in the vault apart from money, I'd have picked myself another bank." For in the bank's safe deposit vault was the Valentino ring.

Can an inanimate object exert a malign influence on those who come into contact with it? All those who have suffered the jinx of Valentino's ring have little doubt that it can. And who can blame them?

Ghostly
Animals

The Case of the Kitten Ghost

I t lies in a special file in the Paris headquarters of the French
Society for Psychical Research—a photograph of a small
boy in his Sunday best, holding a pet kitten in his arms.

The kitten is small and white, with huge, appealing eyes set
in a tiny face. It had been given to seven-year-old René Leret
in August 1954, and from that moment on, the boy and the
little cat were seldom apart. René even took the kitten to
school—at least until the teacher objected. It slept on his bed,
and often sat on his knees at mealtimes

"If anything happens to that cat, I dread to think what René
will do," remarked Michelle Leret to her husband one night.
"It would break the boy's heart."

But when that day came, there was no grief in the cottage
on the edge of the village of Sampier, near Lyons in south-
eastern France. For it seemed that not even death could sepa-
rate René Leret and his pet.

The events at Sampier, at first written off as a small child's fantasies, soon attracted the attention of France's top ghost hunters.

"I have studied well over two thousand cases in the course of my career," wrote Dr. Gerard Lefeve of the French Society of Psychical Research, "and only five times have I failed to put the supernatural into natural terms. One of these was the case of the kitten at Sampier."

It was August in 1954 when René's uncle came to visit, bringing presents for everyone, including the tiny kitten for René. Immediately, the child christened it Jacques, and took it with him everywhere.

But the friendship—at least in normal terms—was to last only a month. One Saturday morning the kitten suddenly dashed through the garden into the main road. An oil truck on its way from Lyons to Dijon dashed the life from the tiny scrap of fur.

The parents kept the boy away from the scene until all traces of the accident were removed. "You must not be too sad about Jacques," Michelle Leret gently told her son. "We will get you another little kitten to take his place."

"I don't need another one, Mother," the boy replied. "Jacques is here sitting by the window." He reached out to stroke the air a few inches above the window ledge.

The parents regarded the action as a defense mechanism shielding René against the grief of losing his pet. Doubtless it would disappear in a couple of days.

But it didn't. Jacques had to have his food put out as usual; the door had to be opened to let him in; the cushion on which he had slept had to be in its place on René's bed.

One day, Charles Leret told his son gently but firmly that the pretense had gone on long enough. The child was bewildered: "But what do you mean? Jacques is here on the carpet—can't you see?"

The next day the worried parents called a doctor and told him their child was suffering from hallucinations. But examinations—culminating in hospital tests—could find nothing mentally wrong with the child.

Dr. Lefeve, hearing of the phenomenon, arrived at the village at the end of September. He had several long interviews with the child and his parents, and he carried out several routine tests. He found that when the child entered the room, the temperature appeared to drop slightly—always a sign of a "presence." Examining the inside of the front door, he found minute scratches around the bottom, apparently made by cat claws. Yet the door had been newly painted—after the cat had died.

Then there was the photograph. Dr. Lefeve was in the Leret house when it came back from the local pharmacy. The folder containing prints from a roll of film taken by Charles Leret was opened and the contents casually examined. There were pictures of the house, the family, and the garden.

And there was a picture of René, taken near the garden gate. Charles Leret's hand shook as he handed the picture to the doctor. It showed René, in his best clothes, looking strangely solemn. In his arms was a white kitten.

"The parents were astonished," Dr. Lefeve recalls. "When the photo was taken, there was no kitten or anything else in the child's arms. I examined the photograph and there was no doubt that the object was a kitten.

"I asked the parents every question I could think of, and they answered willingly and honestly, but they could not throw any light on the mystery."

And no one ever has. For the picture of René Leret had been taken three weeks after Jacques the kitten had died.

A Horse Named Lady Wonder

The two men could barely keep a straight face as the stable door opened and out shuffled the oldest, boniest horse they had ever seen. This clinched it! Now there was no mistake: The whole thing was a hoax.

On the face of it, the feelings of the men who stood in the stable yard in St. John's, Newfoundland, Canada, in 1955, would have been echoed by anyone with normal healthy skepticism. For they had been persuaded, despite their better judgment, to seek advice from this pathetic creature on the fate of a missing child.

But within minutes, what appeared to be a joke in rather bad taste was transformed into an uncanny glimpse into the supernatural that no one has ever been able to explain.

It soon became obvious that only one being in the whole of Canada knew what had happened to three-year-old Ronnie Weitcamp. And that was Lady Wonder, a thirty-year-old mare, spending the twilight of her days in a stable a hundred miles away.

On October 11, 1955, Ronnie left his three playmates in the front yard of his home near a Newfoundland naval base and ran around to the back of the house. He disappeared into some nearby woods and, despite the pleas of his playmates, wouldn't come out. As they ran to tell his mother, the child roamed deeper into the woods.

Neighbors scoured the woodland. By mid-afternoon, the police had been called and a full-scale search mounted. As darkness fell, 1,500 searchers combed bushes and ravines. The bitter cold descended. They knew that if the child was not found, there was little chance of his surviving the night.

But he wasn't found, and the police, convinced that their search had been thorough, turned to other theories. Had he been kidnapped? Eleven days passed, and there was no sign of the child.

The tips and leads supplied by the public led to nothing, and hope was almost abandoned. Then a police official remembered that a child had been found years before, through information supplied by a horse!

In any other circumstance it would have been laughable, but the police looking for little Ronnie Weitcamp had become desperate. Just as the searchers were nearly defeated by despair, two detectives were sent to interview the horse.

By any standards, Lady Wonder was a remarkable horse. By the time she was two years old she had learned to count and spell out words by moving children's blocks around.

One day she spelled out "engine" as a huge tractor rumbled past the house. Later, in response to questions, the horse would use her nose to flip up large tin letters that hung from a bar across her stall. In this way, she spelled out the answers to questions put to her.

The fame of the horse had spread. Thousands came to seek answers to their queries. She was claimed to have predicted that Franklin D. Roosevelt would be the next president of the United States, before he had even been nominated.

She picked the winners of countless races, and venturing into the field of mathematics, briskly calculated the cube roots of numbers. University specialists in extrasensory perception spent weeks testing the horse and came away convinced that she had some kind of telepathic powers.

But she remained basically a harmless curiosity until one day, after a four-month search for a seven-year-old girl, the police turned in desperation to Lady Wonder. She directed them to a water-filled quarry that already had been searched without success. A further hunt led to the child's body, exactly where the horse had indicated.

Coincidence or not, in the absence of any other idea it was worth trying. But now the horse was old and such tests upset her. After convincing the owner that this was an emergency, the officers were eventually allowed to question Lady Wonder.

The bar of letters was put in place and the questions began. They asked, "Do you know why we are here?" Immediately the horse spelled out "boy."

Q: Do you know the boy's name?
A: Ronnie.
Q: Is he dead or alive?
A: Dead.
Q: Was he kidnapped?
A: No.
Q: Will he be found?
A: Yes.
Q: Where?
A: Hole.
Q: What is near him?
A: Elm.
Q: What kind of soil?
A: Sand.
Q: When will he be found?
A: December.

That was the end of the interview. Refusing to answer any further questions, the mare tottered away. The detectives telephoned headquarters with the answers and a new search was discussed.

A storm of ridicule descended as it became known the police were acting on the advice of a horse. Naval base officials, particularly, insisted that the ground had been thoroughly searched and it was quite obvious that the child had been abducted. However, a new search took place, nothing was found, and the police department began to curse the day they sought the help of Lady Wonder.

Then on the afternoon of Sunday, December 4, the body of Ronnie Weitcamp was found by two boys in a thicket at the bottom of a ravine about a mile from his home. He had not been kidnapped: Medical evidence showed he had died of exposure. He lay in sandy soil, just out of the shade of the nearest tree—a large elm.

Every detail of the horse's prediction had been proved uncannily accurate; it was unbelievable but true. It was also the last time Lady Wonder used the swinging letters. The following spring, she died, taking with her the mystery of her glimpse into a world few humans have ever penetrated.

Ghost Dog on the Stairway

A ghost dog was seen in 1929, not once but several times, and not only by humans but by dogs as well. One human who saw it was Pierre van Paassen, world-famous author of *Days of Our Years*.

In the spring of that year, van Paassen was living in Bourg-en-Forêt in France. One night he was startled to see a black dog pass him on the stairs of the house in which he was staying. It reached the landing and disappeared.

Van Paassen searched the house, but could not find any sign of the dog. He assumed it must have been a stray that had wandered in and out again.

A few days later he left on a short trip, not thinking much more about the dog on the stairway. When he returned, however, he found the household greatly upset. During his absence several others had also seen the black dog, always on the stairs.

Van Paassen decided to stake out and watch for the ghostly animal the following night. For corroborating witnesses, he invited a neighbor, Monsieur Grevecoeur, and his young son to join him.

Sure enough, the same black dog appeared at the head of the stairs. Grevecoeur whistled, as he would at any ordinary dog. The dog wagged its tail in friendly fashion.

The three men started up the stairs. To their amazement the black animal began to fade and it vanished before they could reach it.

A few evenings later van Paassen stood watch again, this time accompanied by two police dogs. Once more the ghostly canine appeared, and this time came partway down the stairs before it vanished.

A moment later the two police dogs seemed to be engaged in a death struggle with an invisible adversary, and presently one of the huge dogs fell to the floor dead. Examination failed to reveal any outward signs of injury.

This was too much for the owner. He called in a priest to advise him. The Abbé de la Roudaire arrived and watched with van Paassen the next night. When the black dog appeared the priest stepped toward it. The beast gave a low growl and faded away once more.

The Abbé at once asked the owner of the house if there was a young girl employed there. The owner admitted that there was, but also wanted to know why the priest had asked. Did the good Abbé think that there might be some connection between the young girl and the mysterious apparition?

The Abbé shrugged his shoulders and said there was sometimes an affinity between young people and some types of mysterious happenings. The girl was dismissed—and the ghost dog on the stairs was never seen again.

5

What's in the House

The Thing in the Cellar

This ghost tale from New Jersey may illustrate the moral that if you happen to have a ghost in your house, the most practical course of action is to be hospitable. It might even pay off in hard cash...

It seems that a house in Trenton had been known to be haunted for many years, and nobody would rent it, in spite of its being an attractive little cottage in a nice neighborhood. Finally a local man with a rather bad reputation appeared and offered to take it over. The owner informed him of the house's reputation and detailed its history. The man was not at all fazed. He laughed and signed the lease, saying he wasn't afraid of man, monster, or ghost.

One night, after living in the house about a week, the tenant had to go into the cellar. He took a candle and headed down. He was two steps above its stone floor when a huge black "thing" rose up at the bottom of the stairs. It had two glowing yellow-white eyes that seemed to stare clear through him. The man was startled but instead of fleeing he swore at the phantom and hurled his candlestick at it.

The neighbors found him a day or so later. He was alive, but all his hair was burned off, and he was a mass of bruises from head to toe. He moved out as soon as he was able to.

The next tenant was a gentle elderly lady who did a great deal of work for the local church. She had heard about the phantom, but the little house was inexpensive and it suited her, and she decided to move in, ghost or no ghost. She would take her chances, she said. It was lucky for her that she did.

After several days in the house with no disturbance, she too had to go to the cellar after dark. As the gleam of the candle lit up the stone cellar, the gruesome thing rose up before her. She held the candle higher and said very calmly, "My, you startled me, my friend, but what in the name of heaven do you want? Is

there anything I can do to help you, as long as we are going to
live here together?"

To her astonishment the black shape motioned for the lady
to follow. It slowly drifted back across the stone flagging of the
floor to an old wooden chest in the corner. She followed with
the candle and obeyed the directions of the "thing" when it
motioned for her to move the chest aside. It was empty, and she
moved it easily. She found a loose flagstone underneath. The
murky figure motioned for her to lift the flagstone, and again,
she complied.

Underneath it was a lead-lined box full of old gold coins.
She stared at them for a moment. Then, half to herself, she
said, "Can these be for me?" and turned to look at the
phantom. It was gone, but a cool breeze touched her on the
cheek in an almost friendly caress.

The Headless Lady

Charles Needham, recovering from an illness, rented a small cottage on the edge of the charming town of Canewdon in Southeast Essex, England. The year was 1895 and Needham was settling down to convalesce. The housekeeper he hired for day work seemed concerned that he was planning to sleep in the cottage alone. She kept asking if he thought he would be "all right." He assured her that as far as he knew, he would be, and for two or three nights he was. Then something happened.

He was sitting and reading in the kitchen one midnight, when he was startled by a click of the door latch behind him. The door led to a backyard garden. He watched the latch lift and then slowly fall again. The door was securely bolted at top and bottom, and whoever it was outside did not try to push against it. Needham remembered that the front door was unbolted and hurried into the other room. As he slid the bolt home, the latch of that door too began to rise to the top of the slot. It hesitated a moment and then slowly dropped back into place.

Needham was sick with tuberculosis and not a fit match for an intruder. Nevertheless, he slid back the bolt and threw open the door. There was no one there. For several nights this continued, much to Needham's discomfort, but he decided not to mention the matter either to his housekeeper or to any of the townspeople. He was a lawyer from London and suspected that youngsters in the neighborhood might be having a little cruel fun with him. He would withstand their pranks, he decided. But a few weeks later he had to change his mind...

He had been visiting a friend in town, a chess-playing doctor, and his host had offered to drive him back to the cottage in his pony cart. They were jogging up to the entrance of the little lane leading to the cottage when suddenly the pony stopped and refused to go farther, in spite of blows from the whip. Needham explained it was only a short walk anyway and got out, thanking his friend for the lift.

As he hurried home, he saw a small light ahead of him along one side of the moonlit road. The trees were thick in that section. Needham assumed the light was a lantern held by another pedestrian on the way home, so he quickened his step to catch up.

A few yards farther on, the figure ahead stepped out into the moonlight, close by his cottage, stood a few moments, and then turned toward him. Needham turned and fled in terror. The figure was a woman, but a woman without a head! Needham ran all the way to the "Chequers," a small inn down the road.

He gave a babbled description of what he had seen, and was amazed to learn that the headless lady was a well-known Canewdon resident who had been murdered and decapitated by her husband many years before. She had once lived in the cottage he had rented. Perhaps she had been trying to enter and set up housekeeping again when she found the doors bolted against her.

Needham slept at the inn that night. The next day, he moved.

The Ghost of Greylock

I can vouch for this ghost-sighting personally. It happened to me.

I once hunted fairly regularly in Massachusetts with a friend named Dick Davis. On one trip, Davis and I decided to work our way up the slopes of Mt. Greylock, in the northwestern corner of the state between Adams and North Adams. Mt. Greylock isn't huge (3,506 feet), but it is rugged, and there were plenty of white-tailed deer browsing on its slopes.

We slept the first night in a haymow and went off separately the next morning. We planned to meet late in the afternoon at a deserted farmhouse we saw upon the slope.

About mid-afternoon I was hunting along the edge of a swamp when I was startled to hear the shrill blast of a police whistle through the brush. I knew I hadn't passed any red lights, so I waited to see what was coming. It turned out to be an old fellow who lived in the area and was hunting rabbits with an eager beagle. The whistle was to call the pup. We got to talking and I mentioned my plan to meet Davis at the old farmhouse later. The hunter looked at me sharply.

"Wouldn't go there, son!" he said. "Better meet your friend out in front."

When I asked him why I shouldn't go into the old house, he mumbled something about "bad flooring," then picked up his shotgun and left with the pup at his heels.

When I got to the farmhouse later, however, I did go in and decided to wait in one of the upstairs rooms. It overlooked an orchard where a few apples might still attract a deer. I settled down to wait. The floors and stairs seemed firm enough to me, even if the old building was run-down, long deserted, and had a corner of its roof missing.

About a half-hour after I'd arrived, I heard Dick climb the porch steps, knock snow and mud from his boots, and come in. I decided to keep still and give him a bit of a scare should he start up the stairs. I heard him walking around down below, opening and shutting the old cupboard doors. Then he came to the foot of the stairs just below the room in which I was squatting by the window. He started up and I expected to see his red knitted cap appear over the top step any second. It didn't appear. Perhaps he had seen my muddy tracks and decided to surprise me, I thought. He was waiting on the stairs. Okay, I'd outwait him.

A half-hour later I still was crouching by the window, waiting. I hadn't heard another sound from the person on the stairs, and by now I was in a rather nervous state, even if I did have a loaded shotgun in my hands. Suddenly a movement in the orchard below caught my eye. It was Dick!

Gun ready, I rose and crept out of the room. The stairs were deserted. I rushed out of the house to meet Dick and never went back in. I've often wondered who or what had started up those old stairs to where I waited, and then changed its mind, for as I hurried out of the house I noticed there were no other tracks but mine on the faded yellow floor.

The Haunted Cleaning Lady

Ghosts abound on Nantucket Island, off the coast of Massachusetts, as they do on many places near the water. One theory is that the damp atmosphere makes it easier for spirits to transfer their energy to us living people. "The mind is electrical," is the way one psychic puts it, "and what is the best conductor of electricity? Water."

But although Margo Smith, as a native of Nantucket, was no stranger to ghosts and stories of ghosts, when she took the job of cleaning Mrs. Deauville's house, it got to be just too much, although she stuck it out for quite a while. Her employer was away a lot, so during Margo's weekly cleaning chores she usually was alone in the house.

"On my first day at work," Margo recalls, "I brought my dog with me. He hopped out of the truck, ran up to the front door, and then wouldn't set foot inside."

He wouldn't go in the front door; he wouldn't go in the back door. She couldn't pull, push or carry him in. He had never done that at any other house. Margo thought to herself, "Oh no, here we go. There's something here."

The spirits—there seemed to be several—started playing with the phone. The first day, Margo was vacuuming when she heard the phone beeping as though someone had just taken it off the hook. She looked, and sure enough, the phone was off the hook.

Okay, she said to herself, I can deal with it. Then, as she was vacuuming, she heard the sound of a group of people, talking and laughing. She turned the vacuum off, and the house was dead silent. She turned the vacuum back on, and the party sounds started again, the high and low voices of women and men talking.

They were just warming up.

After a few weeks, the furniture began to move around. If

Margo was upstairs, she'd hear furniture dragged around downstairs. She'd gallop down the stairs and find that chairs and tables had been moved around.

These things happened only when she was alone in the house, when Mrs. Deauville and her family and guests were somewhere else. Perhaps Margo was a particularly psychic person, whom the spirits knew they could communicate with— and tease.

She never actually saw things being moved—only the results. "I was trying to straighten up and clean," she says, "and they were messing things up as fast as I could put them in order."

Margo never mentioned these happenings to Mrs. Deauville. She left it to her employer to bring up, if she wanted to, and she never did.

The spirits began to step up the pace. One day Margo was vacuuming under a bed, and something grabbed the front of the vacuum. It gave a little, as though something were holding on to it. When Margo pulled hard, the vacuum came loose from the hose and remained under the bed. After a considerable period of debate with herself, Margo worked up the courage to look under the bed. There was nothing there but the vacuum attachment. After another period of convincing herself there was nothing to be afraid of—hah!—Margo forced herself to reach under the bed and grab it.

Margo tried to reason with the ghosts. She'd open the front door and call, "Hello, I'm here. I'll be as quick as I can."

She didn't have much success. Furniture kept moving. Once, after a particularly long period of rumbling, she ran downstairs, to find all the living room chairs arranged in a circle.

Finally it got to be too much, even for Margo, the native Nantuckian. Pictures started coming down off the walls. Dishes clattered in the kitchen. A rug flew through the air and struck Margo in the back. "I also got whacked," says Margo, "by some sofa pillows that zipped across the room on their own. Finally, a chair was thrown at me. It missed me, but that did it!"

Margo resigned.

The Demonic Hairdresser

It's distressing enough to get a bad haircut, but when it's a ghost who is giving it to you, it's an even grimmer experience!

That's what happened to a woman in North Carolina, whom we'll call Mary Johnson. Mary woke up one morning to find that her hair had been cut in a random, haphazard, disfiguring way. Parts of her head looked as though they had been shaved. Then it happened again— and again—sometimes even during the day. Mary would go into a sort of trance—she called it a spell—and when she came to, her hair would be cut.

Mary was about 60, and she lived in a small house with her daughter, Jennifer, who was 30. Jennifer began to wonder if she herself was being possessed by a spirit and was giving her mother these haircuts without knowing it. But sometimes Mary would go into her bedroom and lock the door, even nail it shut, and the haircuts would still occur.

The women began to wonder whether the haircuts were coming from Mary's dead husband, Roger, who was Jennifer's father.

Twenty years before, when the family had been living in Ohio, Roger had become involved in black magic. This terrified Mary, and she took the little girl and fled to North Carolina. Roger was bitterly offended. After a time, he followed and moved in with them. A few years later, he died of a heart attack.

Almost immediately after Roger's death, Mary and Jennifer became aware of strange sounds in the house. They heard knockings, footsteps, and voices whispering. They saw vague, unrecognizable apparitions and soon the haircuts began.

Finally, in desperation, they called in a woman who was both a psychologist and a psychic. Dr. Jeannie Lagle is a well-trained psychotherapist whose work with clients often has an added dimension. She uses her natural psychic abilities to help her clients. She came to the house, talked with the women, and agreed that it was their husband and father who was causing the trouble.

"What we did was a sort of family therapy," Jeannie relates. "The unusual aspect of it was that one of the people—Roger—had been dead for some years."

The three women began meeting in séances, and, according to Jeannie, the spirit of Roger came and joined in. The séances were not an immediate success. Mary got at least one haircut at this time. But eventually the heart-to-heart talks seemed to calm down Roger's fearsome spirit. In the therapy sessions, Jeannie seemed to convince him that by remaining close to the physical plane and harassing his wife he was doing nobody any good, including himself. It seemed that he took Jeannie's advice and went elsewhere.

Whatever happened to Roger, the haircuts stopped!

6

Ghouls on the Move

The Phantom Stagecoach

Many years ago there was a small Arizona frontier town that was kept alive by a nearby gold mine. The town had once been on the stagecoach route, but when the mine petered out and was abandoned, the stage line was discontinued. Now the little town was almost completely cut off from the rest of the settlements. Only a tiny freight line, run infrequently by a local livery stable owner, remained.

One young boy in the poverty-stricken town was always exploring the nearby hills, hoping to find another mine to bring back the people who had moved away. He was also looking for the stagecoach, which he had loved. He had always been there to meet the stagecoach when it came tearing into the little town in a cloud of dust.

The other people in town looked upon the boy's prospecting with amusement, but they did not bother him. In fact, they hoped that he would find a mine and bring prosperity back to the town.

One day the boy left for the hills as usual, with his burro and his lunch, but by nightfall he had not returned. As he had always been back by dark before, his folks became concerned. True, he was self-reliant and used to the rough living of the times and the area, but anything might have happened.

Finally, just after midnight, he came home, exhausted but excited. The stagecoach, he said, had come back to town after all. Then he told this story.

He had become separated from his burro back in the hills, and after searching for a long time, he gave up and started home on foot. It was dark by the time he reached the old coach road to town, and he could hear the howls of wolves in the timber of the foothills close by.

He hurried, but the cries of the wolves behind him became louder and louder. In panic he climbed to the top of a high rock

by the roadside to wait for the pack to close in. Just as the wolves approached, he heard the noise of a stagecoach coming along the old road. A huge stagecoach drawn by black, shining horses pulled around the bend and came to a leather-creaking stop beside the rock where the boy clung in terror. The driver motioned for him to climb in, and the coach raced toward town with the wolves howling right behind.

His parents had trouble believing the boy's story. No one had seen the stagecoach in years, and the boy was known to have an active imagination. But the strangest part was to come to light the next day.

Just outside of town, a huge grey wolf was found, obviously run over by a heavy wagon or stagecoach. The tracks of the vehicle came right to the edge of town, and then they stopped. They did not turn around and go back—they just stopped, as though they had vanished with the coach that made them.

Something had brought the boy back to safety—and it was certainly more substantial than imagination.

The Runaway Locomotive

In January of 1892 engineer J. M. Pinkney visited his friend, a seasoned engineer on the old Northern Pacific Eastbound Overland train. Pinkney's friend covered a stretch of track that crosses the Cascade Mountains of the northwest United States.

As the friends sat together in the engineer's cab of the locomotive, they regaled each other with harrowing accounts of accidents that had occurred on their lines. Pinkney enjoyed most of the stories, but he couldn't take the ones seriously that featured the paranormal. As hardheaded a man as you could find, he certainly didn't believe in ghosts. As the train neared Eagle Gorge, the most dangerous spot on the 2,500-mile run, the engineer embarked on the story of old Tom Cypher. Cypher, he said, was an engineer who had died in an accident here two years before.

Suddenly, the engineer grasped the throttle and threw it over, reversing the engine. Then he applied the air brakes, bringing the train to a standstill. The spot where he had stopped was just a few feet short of the place where Cypher had met his death.

Pinkney couldn't understand why the engineer had stopped the train. There had been no hint of any danger. The night was clear and the track was empty. The engineer explained vaguely that some of the machinery had shaken loose and had to be tightened. In a few minutes, he said, they would be on their way.

As they started forward once more, Pinkney pointed out that there had been nothing wrong with the machinery, so why the stop?

"Look there!" his friend told him. "Don't you see it?"

Staring out of the cab window, Pinkney saw the headlights of a locomotive just 300 yards ahead. Shocked, he automatically reached for the lever to stop the train. His friend pushed his hand away, laughing.

"It's only old Tom Cypher's engine, No. 33," he said. "We won't collide. Because the man at that throttle is Cypher himself and, dead though he may be, he can go faster backwards than any man alive can go forwards. I've seen it 20 times before. Every engineer on this road looks for it."

Pinkney felt the hairs on his neck stand up as he watched the engine ahead of them, its headlights throwing out rays of red, green and white light. It had begun running silently backwards, remaining only a short distance ahead of them. Pinkney glimpsed a shadowy figure at the throttle. Then the locomotive rounded a curve and disappeared from view.

The train on which Pinkney was riding began passing several small stations. At each one, the station master, fearful of an impending collision, warned the engineer to watch out for a runaway engine, No. 33, that was traveling backwards just a short distance ahead of them.

The engineer only laughed. "It's just old Cypher playing a prank," he said.

Pinkney still couldn't believe that a ghost had been at the throttle of that locomotive. Worried, he sent a telegram to the next station, which was in the town of Sprague, asking if No. 33 with a daredevil engineer aboard had been stopped.

The strange reply came back. "Rogue locomotive No. 33 has just arrived, her coal exhausted, her boxes burned out. No engineer at the throttle."

Faces in the Sea

I n January of 1925, a huge oil company tanker was plowing through the Pacific toward the Panama Canal, when tragedy struck. Two men, overcome by gas while cleaning out an empty cargo hatch, were buried at sea.

Several days later a group of greatly disturbed crewmen approached the captain. They told him an astonishing story. They said they had seen both the dead seamen following the ship at twilight the past few nights. The captain refused to take their story seriously, but the reports persisted. Even some of the officers saw the apparition.

The heads of the two men would appear in the water off the side of the ship from which they had been cast and would seem to follow the ship for a few moments. Then they would vanish again. Since so many men had seen the apparitions, the captain finally decided to bring the matter to the attention of the officials of the company when they docked in New Orleans.

The company officers listened, disbelieving at first, then with wonder. One of them suggested that the first mate obtain a camera and be ready for the next appearance of the two ghostly faces in the waves. This was done, and the officer gave the captain a fresh roll of film with orders to keep it sealed until the moment it was to be used. The captain promised he would guard the film.

Back through the canal went the tanker, and out again into the Pacific. And once more, at twilight, as the ship reached the same spot in the ocean, the faces appeared alongside. The captain broke open the film and loaded the camera himself. When the ghosts next appeared, he took six photos and then locked up the camera for safekeeping and away from any possible tampering.

When the ship reached port, the film was taken to a commercial photographer for developing and printing. This man knew nothing about the mystery, nor the reason for the photographs that he processed.

Five of the developed images showed nothing unusual, just waves and spray, but the sixth showed what appeared to be the outlines of two heads and faces in the waves. This photo was enlarged. The objects showed up plainly, appearing in exactly the same relation to the ship as the two ghosts seen by the crewmen and ship's officers.

These photos were eventually inspected by Dr. Hereward Carrington, a noted investigator of psychic phenomena. He checked the story with company officials, and after looking at the photo, reported that there could be no doubt that at least one of the faces in the waves was a realistic photo of one of the dead seamen.

Strange things follow the sea, and not all men go down to the sea in ships. Some wear shrouds.

7

Messages from Beyond

The Ghost of a Deformed Monk

Maurice Maeterlinck was a famous playwright who won the Nobel Prize for literature in 1911. At the time, he was living in France, in a centuries-old building called St. Wandrille Abbey, once inhabited by priests and monks. It had been converted into a private dwelling. It was also reputed to be haunted. This did not bother Maeterlinck, for he was fascinated by ghosts, often referring to them in his works. However, he had never had a ghostly experience in the old abbey, until…

A number of guests were visiting, including the famous Russian actor/director Constantin Stanislavsky. An American woman was staying in another part of the house. In the middle of the night, the occupants were awakened by her screams. As the others gathered, she stammered that she had seen the apparition of a deformed monk.

Maeterlinck was not one to return to bed and let it go at that. Nor were his guests. They immediately made an attempt to communicate with the ghost through table tipping. And they were successful. The table rapped out a message from the spirit who claimed to be a monk named Bertrand.

"Oh save me, save me!" the table tapped out. There was a desperate tone to the message.

The listeners spread out through the building, looking for evidence. Stanislavsky found a plaque on which was inscribed in Latin: "Bertrand: pax vobiscum: AD 1693."

Or, "Peace be with you."

Maeterlinck had heard there was a secret room in the abbey, and the company searched the place, looking for hiding places. Eventually, Maeterlinck found a hollow panel and pushed it open. In a small compartment, they found the bones of a man who had been terribly deformed in life, and who had apparently died there, where he had been walled in.

A Terrifying Visitor

The two young military officers sat in a small apartment, completely unaware of the unusual visitor they were about to have. They were drinking tea, relaxing from their duties. The apartment was part of a British Army barracks in Sydney, Nova Scotia. It was the afternoon of October 15, 1785. They were Lieutenant George Wynyard and Captain John Sherbrooke.

Suddenly Sherbrooke looked up and gasped. Wynyard followed his friend's gaze, and dropped the cup from which he had been sipping. For the two officers saw a young man, about 20, standing at the door. The youth looked very ill. He was dressed in lightweight clothing, despite the cold Nova Scotia weather.

The young man entered the room and walked by the two seated men. Sherbrooke later described the figure as having "the appearance of a corpse." The young man glanced sadly at Wynyard and then, as the officers watched, spellbound, went through the doorway into Wynyard's bedroom.

Wynyard leaped to his feet. "Great heavens," he cried, "that's my brother!"

They rushed into the bedroom, but no one was there.

Communications were slow in those days. It was months later when Wynyard received a letter from India, where his favorite brother, John, had been serving in the British Army. The letter brought the news that John had died—the previous October.

Deadly Kindness

It was after midnight in the hospital ward. The lights were dim. A hospital ward at night can be an eerie place—one of uneasy slumber and the restless movement of people in pain.

On this night in September 1956, the women's ward at one of London's most famous hospitals was to have a most unusual visitor—a ghost on an errand of death.

The Grey Lady of St. Thomas's had visited the hospital over a dozen times since the turn of the century. On nearly every occasion, the patient who saw the apparition died soon afterward.

On the night of September 4, 1956, the night nurse heard a gentle tapping on the outer door of the ward. It was 12:35 a.m. Around her, patients were sleeping. In one corner, in a screened bed, an elderly woman lay gravely and, it was feared, fatally ill. The nurse had been thinking how sad it was that this old lady should die alone with no relatives or friends at her bedside. Then she heard the tapping again, louder this time.

She walked across the room and opened the door. Outside stood a woman dressed in grey. The nurse took her to be a nun. The visitor whispered the name of the dying woman, and the nurse led her to the screened bed. Ten minutes later she looked around the screens that shrouded the corner. There was no one there—except a corpse.

The patient had died.

Puzzled, the nurse asked the night receptionist if she had seen the visitor leave. "What visitor?" was the reply. "No one came to the wards last night."

The nurse telephoned the night porter. He told the same story: "No visitors came through the gates after 9 p.m." The nurse thought she was overtired. Perhaps she had dozed off for a minute and dreamed the incident. But the next morning a patient on the far side of the ward caught her arm as she passed. "Wasn't it nice of the nun to come and sit with that poor soul last night?" the patient remarked.

Since then the Grey Lady has been seen at least six times. And death has followed each visit.

Who is she? She is described as middle-aged and wearing a long grey gown. Some say she is visible only from the ankles upward—because she walks on the level of the wards' floors as they were before the hospital was reconstructed.

Others think she is the ghost of a ward nurse who fell down an elevator shaft at the turn of the century. Still others believe she is the wraith of a head nurse who was found dead in her office on the top floor. But most popular is the belief that she is the ghost of "Morphine Lizzie." Lizzie Church, a nurse at the hospital, had been looking after her fiancé, who had been admitted after an accident, when she accidentally gave him a fatal dose of morphine. Now she is said to appear whenever desperately ill patients are given morphine injections.

Most nurses have a healthy respect for hospital taboos and superstitions. Some will not put red and white flowers together in a vase. To do so, they say, means a death in the ward. And others won't allow white lilies in a patient's room. There is an old hospital belief that they too lead to death.

But not too many of St. Thomas's Hospital nurses believed in the tales of the Grey Lady until one day in 1947. Throughout that afternoon, four nurses working in the women's ward all glanced, at various times, behind a screen that separated off a seriously ill patient. They all saw a nun and two elderly people talking to the woman.

One of the nurses told the head nurse that the patient had visitors, and the head nurse said angrily that she had not given anyone permission to be there. She went to the ward and found the patient dead, a peaceful smile on her lips—and no sign of visitors.

Later one of the nurses going through the dead woman's effects with a relative saw a small gold locket. Inside were two photographs of a couple she instantly recognized. They were the elderly people she had seen with the nun.

"But that's not possible," said the mystified relation. "They are her father and mother—they both died years ago."

On another occasion, a patient in a men's ward at St. Thomas's looked up, surprised as the young night nurse picked up his water jug. "There's no need to fill it, nurse," he said. "That nice lady in grey has just given me a glass of water." The man pointed to the foot of the bed. The nurse looked but there was no one there. She did not argue. She knew what happened to people who claimed to see the ghost dressed in grey. The patient, not seriously ill, took a sudden and inexplicable turn for the worse. He died the next day, twenty-four hours to the minute after the Grey Lady had offered her deadly kindness.

A Lady's Reign of Death

Three people in the village of Bryanston, near Blandford in Dorset, saw the Lady in White during one long, hot summer, and they lived but briefly to tell the tale. No one knew whether the Lady in White was real or not; it's doubtful if they ever will. One thing they did know for certain was that she was the harbinger of death.

Early in May, at dusk, farmworker Robert Crewe was walking home when a tall woman dressed in white stopped him in a narrow lane.

"I am looking for the house of Robert Crewe," she told him. "I have a message for him."

"Then you're in luck," he replied, "for I am the man."

"As I said that," Crewe told his wife later, "the lane seemed to suddenly grow dark, and the woman disappeared."

Three days later, Robert Crewe was kicked to death by a horse he was grooming in a stable, and the Lady in White's reign of terror began.

John Allen, a keeper on an estate near Blandford, spent most of the summer with two other men cutting weeds in the River Stour. He was a cheerful and kindly man, but one night in July he came home from his work and cried bitterly for more than an hour.

His wife, trying to comfort him, asked what was the matter, and Allen replied that he had seen a sign that made him sure he didn't have long to live. He refused to say what he had seen, but remained in low spirits for the rest of the week. He went to work as usual the next day and nothing happened. Eventually, thinking he had been mistaken, he regained some of his good humor and life in the Allen family returned to normal.

The Allens had two daughters, Mary, age six, and Polly, three. At the beginning of August, Polly had been playing in the front yard before she ran into her house with some strange news.

"There was a tall lady in a white dress coming down the hill opposite," she said. "She asked me where my father was and I said he was at the river."

Curious to know who the stranger was, Mrs. Allen went out front. There was no one there. The road leading to the village was empty. Mrs. Allen remarked to her sister, who had come for tea, "Polly must have imagined it—whoever saw a woman dressed in white in these parts on a workday?"

But the child insisted that she had been spoken to by a woman who was "terribly tall, much taller than you, Mother."

As Polly went back out to play, Mrs. Allen glanced at the clock. It was 4 PM. She put on the kettle and set the table for tea. At that precise moment, the body of John Allen was floating lifelessly in the River Stour.

With two companions named Elforde and Ball, he had been standing in the river cutting weeds from the bank when he slipped and fell into a deep, mud-filled hole in the riverbed. By the time his companions found his body, John Allen was dead. They took the body to a nearby church, and the priest broke the news to Allen's family.

When told of her husband's death, Mrs. Allen immediately said to her sister, "That must have been poor John's spirit that Polly saw."

The rest of the village did not agree with this view. They were convinced the apparition was the Lady in White, the malevolent being who brought death to all who saw her. Their conviction was certainly strengthened when, on September 4, Polly Allen was fatally injured by the moving wheels of a farm cart, into which she ran while playing in the village street.

8

Tales
of Terror

The Terrible Hand

I 1917, Mrs. Roy Jackson, of Harrison, New York, went to live in Paterson, New Jersey, with her young husband. They had little money for rent, but they stumbled on an extremely inexpensive house, even for those days.

Mrs. Jackson felt uneasy about the house and at first wanted no part of it, even at twelve dollars a month. Mrs. Jackson's brother, a lawyer who examined the lease, remarked on the dwelling's vaguely sinister atmosphere—saying that he felt a "presence" there that was "not good"—but the rent was low, so the Jacksons moved in.

The months went by and Mrs. Jackson's apprehension grew. Then one day she learned from neighbors that the house was so cheap because it was supposed to be haunted. A distraught mother had killed herself and her two children in the house several years before. Since then no one had stayed longer than a few days. There were rumors that one of the tenants, and perhaps even more, had been found dead after shrieking, "Someone has me by the throat."

Roy Jackson scoffed at the yarns. He insisted they stay on in spite of his wife's feeling that she was constantly being peered at, followed, and warned to move. Then, on an October night his young wife came face to face with terror and almost lost her life.

The first World War had come, and Roy had begun to talk of enlisting. Mrs. Jackson was lying on a sofa in the living room, thinking about the changes the war would make in her life and looking at a bright spot on the ceiling—a reflection from the gas fixture on the table, she thought. Suddenly she was aware of a second bright spot on the ceiling. Perhaps light from outside? A reflection from a mirror? But there was no other light or mirror.

The spot grew and grew, writhing like "thousands of cobwebs turning and twisting into a mass." A point protruded from the whirling mass, then another and another until she recognized it as a hand with five long, pointed fingers.

Suddenly the mass stopped whirling. Then it grew a long wispy arm behind the fingers, and the entire phantasm darted down from the ceiling, seizing Mrs. Jackson by the throat. With an agonizing lurch, she hurled herself to the floor and lay on the rug, face down, gasping for breath. Moments later she forced herself out of the room to the stairs.

Shaken but unhurt, she finally convinced her husband they should move. One encounter with the grey whirling terror had been enough.

Years later, out of curiosity, the Jacksons returned to Paterson and visited their former landlady. She was in great pain from an old injury. She said that after the Jacksons left, the house had been rented to a single woman. One night she heard screaming and ran up to help—but found her tenant struggling on the floor, choking to death. In her terror, she grabbed the landlady, tearing ligaments that never healed.

What Got Oliver Larch?

It happened in 1889 on Christmas Eve. The setting was a farm near South Bend, Indiana. Four or five inches of snow covered the yards and the henhouse roof. Eleven-year-old Oliver Larch lived on the farm with his parents, who were giving a Christmas party for some old friends of the family—a minister and his wife, and an attorney from Chicago.

After dinner, they gathered around a pump organ, and Mrs. Larch played carols while the others sang. She played "Silent Night" and "The Twelve Days of Christmas." Warm voices filled the cozy room, and laughter. After a while, Oliver went to the kitchen to pop corn on the wood-burning range.

At this point, his father noticed that the grey granite bucket used for drinking water was almost empty. He asked Oliver to run out to the well in the yard and refill it. The boy set aside his corn-popper and put on his overshoes. It was just a few minutes before eleven o'clock. It would soon be Christmas, and he wanted to get back to the party quickly.

His father returned to the living room to add his voice to the chorale, as Oliver stepped out into the night—and eternity.

About a dozen seconds after he had left the doorway, the adults around the organ were stunned by screams from the yard. They rushed out the same door Oliver had used. Mrs. Larch grabbed up a kerosene lamp to light the way.

Outside, the dark, starless night was filled with scream after scream of, "Help! Help! They've got me! They've got me!"

What made the adults recoil in horror was that Oliver's screams were coming from high above them in the blackened sky. The piercing cries grew fainter and fainter, and finally faded away completely as the stunned group stared at each other in speechless disbelief.

The men sprang to life, seized the lamp, and followed the youngster's tracks toward the well. They did not get far.

Halfway to the well, roughly 30 feet from the house, the tracks abruptly ended. No signs of a scuffle or struggle, just the end of the tracks. They found the heavy stone bucket about 15 feet to the left of the end of the tracks, dropped in the snow as though from above. That was all.

Oliver had started straight for the well, and then had been carried away—by what? He was too heavy for a large bird, or even several birds, to lift. He was a big boy, weighing about 75 pounds. Airplanes had not yet been invented. No balloons were aloft that night.

Who, or what, seized Oliver Larch? It remains a mystery that has not been solved to this day, and probably never will be.

The Boy with the Brass Buttons

The old-fashioned house in Stuyvesant Square caught the eye of a young couple who had just arrived in Philadelphia on a winter day in 1889. They bought it and moved in with their little six-year-old daughter.

There was a lot of refurbishing to be done, so it was nice to have an attic in which the little girl could play while the rest of the house was being worked on. The previous owners, the Cowderys, had turned the attic into a playroom. It even had a fireplace, though it was now boarded up.

After a couple of weeks, the downstairs rooms were finished. The mother, realizing she hadn't seen much of her daughter in the past fortnight, planned to spend more time with her. But the little girl wasn't interested. She kept stealing away to the attic.

"What's so interesting up there in that stuffy room?" the exasperated mother asked at last.

"It's the little boy with the shiny buttons," the child replied. "He's so much fun to play with."

"What little boy?" her mother demanded, wondering if a servant's child had somehow stowed away in the room. She went to investigate. But the room was empty.

Certain that her daughter was just being stubborn, the mother appealed to her husband to discipline the child. At her father's stern voice, the little girl became hysterical. She kept repeating that there was a little boy and that he wore a blue jacket with lots of shiny buttons on it.

As her father listened, he became more and more curious. Formerly a seaman, he recognized her description of the buttons. They were probably brass and part of a child's sailor suit.

He then made some inquiries about the Cowderys, the

family who had lived in the house before him. He learned that they had come from England with their children, two boys and a girl. The youngest child, a boy, was retarded. The neighbors described him as an idiot child. According to the neighbors, the young boy had always loved the nearby river. One day he had sneaked away on his own to play on its banks. He had fallen into the water and drowned. His body was never recovered, but his cap had been found floating on the river. Shortly after the child's disappearance, the Cowderys put the house up for sale and, leaving Philadelphia, dropped out of sight.

The former seaman's suspicions were now thoroughly aroused. He accompanied his little daughter to the attic and asked her to show him where the boy came from. She pointed to the boarded-up fireplace. Her father called in workers to open it and then to remove the mortar that cemented up a cavity in the wall beside the chimney.

As the mortar was chipped away, the corpse of a small boy was revealed. He was clothed in a little blue sailor jacket with four rows of brass buttons down the front. Examination showed that the back of the child's skull had been crushed.

No accidental drowning! Cold-blooded murder!

9
Stranger Than Fiction

The Old Man of the Woods

Presque Isle, Maine—one of the most remote spots in the United States—is perhaps for this reason the setting for many peculiar legends and tales. One resident reported the following weird incident during World War II.

Near the spot where this man's father had lived when he was a boy, there later lived a Presque Isle family with two children—a boy and a girl. The youngsters had no friends to play with in the deserted area, so they had to invent their own games and entertainment. They often took walks in the nearby woods.

One day the children began to talk about a nice old man who lived in a cabin back over the hills. At first, the parents were concerned. But no one knew of any such man, nor could his cabin be found. They decided the old man had been dreamed up by the children to make up for their lack of real friends—so they didn't give the matter much thought.

As time went on, the children began to report on some things that the old man said would be happening to the local residents, their livestock, and their crops. Strangely enough, almost all these dire events took place.

People lost their crops, their livestock died, and folks were taken sick—just as the children's friend had said they would.

The parents of the youngsters didn't approve of the morbid interest in death and destruction their children were displaying. And so, the children were refused permission to visit the woods anymore, although they continued to sneak away whenever they could.

Finally the parents delivered an ultimatum: The children would bring the old man home to meet their family, or they would be forbidden ever to see him again.

The boy and the girl said they would invite their friend, but they were not sure he would come. Off they went into the woods, with the parents laughing as they waited—assuming there was no such person at all, but marveling at how their offspring could have departed so full of confidence.

They soon found out.

A half-hour later, the children returned. A tall bearded man—obviously very old, but with a strong, active stride—was with them. He was strangely dressed, in a suit of black material that had twinkling glints of gold here and there. His battered hat appeared to be made of a special black fur felt. His beard was pure white, and his blue eyes were piercing.

He greeted the parents pleasantly, and they were soon reassured that their children had indeed found an interesting and unusual friend. After staying for a while, the old man bade them farewell and asked if the boy and girl could walk back with him to the edge of the woods to say good-bye. The parents agreed, and the three started off, the man holding the youngsters by their hands.

As the little band walked toward the sunset, the parents were startled to see that only the children cast a shadow—there was none for the bearded man who walked between them. Their awareness came too late, however.

Neither the old man nor the children were ever seen again.

The Hunter and the Hunted

The ghost of an elephant control officer is often seen roaming in the bush in Zimbabwe, some 20 miles from Serenje. It's as if he is still doing his duty: Hunting down rogue elephants and keeping them away from the farm country.

Although it was Richard James' job to kill the great beasts, he made no secret of the fact that he had an enormous respect—even affection—for the elephants. He frequently spoke of them as the gentlemen of the jungle, wise, courteous and affectionate, and said that when he had to die, he only hoped that he would be killed by an elephant. He got his wish.

On one of his tours from his base at Serenje, he penetrated deep into the bush, chasing a rogue elephant. When he caught up with it, he hit the elephant with his first shot, but failed to kill it. Then, when the wounded and infuriated animal charged him, his gun misfired. Everything happened so quickly that his bearers were unable to shoot before the animal reached Richard and hurled him into a tree.

After the elephant was killed, his bearers climbed the tree and gently brought Richard back to the ground. They carried him a short way, but his back was broken and he knew he was dying. His final request was to be buried at the spot where he had fallen. He wanted to stay in the bush country forever.

His bearers soon prepared a grave, and after a short burial ceremony made the long trek back to Serenje, where they reported the tragic accident.

The story should have ended there. But when the news of Richard's death eventually reached officialdom, whoever received it failed to understand the significance of the dead man's request. A month later, a special expedition was sent to exhume his body and take it back to the European cemetery at Mpika, near Serenje.

But when the expedition arrived, the grave was surrounded by elephants. Each time someone moved in the direction of the grave, the elephants became angry and charged.

Two days passed; a number of elephants were killed, and eventually the body was recovered and the expedition went back to Mpika.

John Littler was appointed to be Richard's replacement, and six weeks after the funeral he heard that elephants in that area were causing a great deal of disturbance and damage. He decided to go back to the place where the accident had occurred, but had great difficulty persuading his bearers to go with him. It was as if they had a premonition of what was about to happen.

The party was within 100 yards of the original grave when one of the bearers gave a terrible scream, dropped the supplies he was carrying, and ran back along the path. He was quickly followed by all the native bearers. Littler and his assistant stood alone, surrounded by supplies that lay where the bearers had dropped them as they fled.

Then both men saw the cause of the panic. For there, standing near the grave, surrounded by a large herd of elephants, was Richard James. Littler knew that it could not be James. He had helped to bury his colleague. It had to be his ghost.

Both men moved forward, and as they did, several elephants lifted their trunks, bellowed, and turned as if to prevent them from reaching the grave.

The ghost seemed to wave them back. It was as if he was warning the two men that if they came any nearer they could easily be killed by the elephants, who by now were very angry indeed.

Littler decided to heed the warning, and the two men retreated, leaving the ghost of Richard James with his beloved elephants. Since 1958, many officials and hunters have reported seeing the ghost within a mile of the spot where he was killed.

Was this a classic case of a man "returning" because of a guilty conscience? Or did he possess a curiously involved relationship with his enemy—the strong affinity that so often exists between the hunter and the hunted?

The Man and the Glove

While sightseeing in Scotland, a young American woman joined a group that was visiting an island where a crumbling castle had recently been opened to the public. As they approached the castle, the young lady noticed that a huge cloud overhead looked like a pair of gauntlet gloves. She called it to the attention of the others in the party, but thought no more about it. The unusual cloud formation soon faded away.

Later that day a sudden and violent storm came up. Because the trip back to the mainland was too rough for their small boat, the sightseers were forced to spend the night at the castle. The young American was given a room in one of the towers. She went to bed quite thrilled at the opportunity to spend the night there.

Awakening during the night, she was surprised to see a pair of white gauntlets on the floor by her bed. The gloves were surrounded by a halo of light that illuminated a crest embroidered in red silk. As the bewildered woman raised her eyes from the strange sight, she was even more startled to see a tall, dark young man looking at her from the shadows beyond the gloves. At her gasp of terror, both the glowing gloves and the young man vanished.

Perhaps, she thought, it had been a dream, inspired by the gauntlet-shaped cloud she had seen earlier. She didn't mention her ghostly visitor to anyone.

Several years passed. In New York, she met a young Scotsman and married him. Shortly after their honeymoon, he received word that a maiden aunt had died in New England, and the newlyweds had to go there to close the house. It was very run-down and dilapidated, with hardly a sign that it had been lived in. The young bride occupied herself by poking about the attic. There in an old trunk, neatly wrapped in a bit of tartan, was a pair of white gauntlets, exactly the same as those she had seen in the castle years before.

She hurried downstairs in excitement to show them to her husband and tell him about the strange coincidence. When she held them out to him, he turned deathly pale. "So, my dear," he said, "you were the girl in the bed that night!" Then he vanished—for the second time! His bride fainted, and when she came to, she was alone. Questioning the neighbors later, she was told that no one had lived in the old house for a hundred years. She never saw her husband again.

The Spell on the Mirror

In the War Memorial Hospital at Sault Ste. Marie, Michigan, Jefferey Derosier was close to death. He knew he was critically ill, and so did the three other patients who shared the small ward.

One afternoon Derosier asked the nurse to hand him the small mirror from the enamel table beside his bed. The nurse gave him the mirror, which was just a plain piece of silvered glass without a frame or handle.

A moment later he threw it back upon the bedside table and cried hysterically, "I'm dying!" The other patients, watching him, were stunned. He spoke again in a low, dull voice. "You won't be able to pick up that mirror," he said. Then he died.

After his body had been removed, one of the other patients casually tried to pick up the mirror. He couldn't budge it from where it lay on the white table. Baffled, he asked the nurse to pick it up, but she couldn't move it either. A doctor was called, and he too tried to lift the mirror from its place. It would not move.

Soon word of the "haunted" mirror spread throughout the hospital. Nurses, interns, and curious patients all tried to move the little mirror from where the dying man had thrown it. No one succeeded. All day the mirror defied every attempt to move it. Even when a nurse tried to pry it loose with an ice pick, it remained sealed to the tabletop.

Then another nurse tried to work her fingernail under the edge of the little piece of glass. As if at that moment the spell was broken, the mirror flew several feet into the air and fell to the floor unbroken. At last it had moved.

Trying to find a reason for the mirror sticking to the table as long as it had, some of the witnesses attempted to make it stick again. But they couldn't do it. There was no adhesive on the back of the piece of silvered glass and anyone could now pick it up easily from the dry tabletop. They wet the surface in an attempt to create suction so that the mirror would stick once more, but the spell was broken.

Later the mirror was cracked, perhaps on purpose, and thrown away. There was never any explanation of the spell cast by Jefferey Derosier's dying words.

10

Spirited Encounters

Death at the Falls

T here is a long slim gravestone on the American side of Niagara Falls commemorating those who met their deaths in the raging whirlpool below the falling cliffs of water. Some died by accident. Others flung themselves over the Falls for fame or money. For others it was a way out of black despair.

A few of them lived for a little while. But Patrick Neil Thompson was not among the elite band. He fell over Niagara Falls one winter night in 1940 and was never seen again—at least not alive.

But how he reappeared two years later, when his son Kenneth was beyond any human aid, is a story that people who live and work within the thunder of the Falls still remember and tell.

Patrick Thompson was a civil engineer. He lived with his wife and son in the small village of Hampstone on the Canadian side of Niagara Falls. In the late 1930s, the Rainbow Bridge, an old suspension bridge connecting the American and Canadian shores some miles up the Niagara River, had been swept away by ice packs. The company that employed Thompson won the major contract to build a new one.

Construction started early in 1939. It was priority work. The Canadians would soon be at war, and every bridge was needed. The men were working in shifts around the clock to replace the Rainbow Bridge. Patrick Thompson was in charge of a team of ten men who were working nights under floodlights on a scaffolding platform in the middle of the Niagara River.

On the night of January 17, 1940, Thompson was supervising the unloading of concrete from a barge into a hopper on the rig. A wind of almost gale force was lashing up from Lake Erie, building the waves on the Niagara River into what looked like oceanic proportions. The string of barges in the darkness below banged and rattled against the rig. Thompson stood guiding the crane bucket into the hopper. Suddenly, the wind caught the crane jib and whipped it savagely to the right. The bucket, at about chest height, caught Thompson, knocking him off the platform into the churning water below.

Five miles downstream the Falls were waiting. He must have been unconscious or semiconscious from the blow because his men heard no sound. Boats were sent out and searchlights raked the water, but Patrick Thompson was never seen again.

An inquest returned a verdict of death by drowning. The coroner expressed sympathy for his widow and son. The company said it was sorry to lose such a fine man. Patrick Thompson died the day before his birthday. He would have been thirty-two years old.

Doris Thompson went back to Hampstone and took a job in the office of a building firm. Her son Kenneth, now ten, was going to the local school.

Two years went by. Mother and son were surviving, and it looked as though they were recovering pretty well from the blow fate had dealt them. But fate, it seemed, had not yet done with the Thompson family.

In early April 1942, Kenneth and two friends were on the bank of the Niagara River. Spring thaw had swollen it into a mile-wide torrent. Huge uprooted trees lurched past in the grip of the relentless current. The boys threw small branches into the water and saw them scud away toward the distant roar of the Falls.

Suddenly, Kenneth Thompson, overwhelmed by enthusiasm for the game, grasped a tree bough and tossed it over the bank. With a scream, he lost his balance and toppled into the stream. His two friends watched transfixed as the boy was whirled away.

Incredibly, he did not drown. He clung to the branch, which, bobbing and rearing like a macabre steed, swept him steadily toward the Falls and destruction. His friends, shocked into action, ran to their bicycles and made for the nearest telephone.

The boatmen at Horseshoe Falls prepared their rescue vessels and lifelines but they knew it was hopeless. Water at least forty feet thick was hurling itself over the four-hundred-foot-high curve of rock. Spray lashed hundreds of feet into the air. No human life could persist amid such fury.

Kenneth, on the last bend before the Falls, felt the branch on which he rode speed up like a powerful car. He struggled to keep his head above water. His numb fingers slipped off the bark, and the branch jerked free of him. As Kenneth sank deeply into the blinding waters, he felt in his heart that he would never rise again. Straight ahead, he could see the semicircular outline of the edge of the Falls and knew the end was only seconds away.

Then it happened. He felt arms closing around his shoulders. No longer was he drifting helplessly on the current. He could feel the water surging against him, but he was no longer moving. Firmly held by some unknown, unseen force, he began to move toward the bank.

Then he heard the voice. It was low, soft, and heartbreakingly familiar. "Hold on to me and don't be afraid," it said. "I will take care of you."

It was the voice of his father. Of that, Kenneth Thompson had no doubt. Nor had he any doubt that some tangible presence supported him on the hundred-yard fight against the current and helped him up the bank to safety. *Because Kenneth Thompson could not swim.*

The Fourth Presence

When Sir Ernest Shackleton wrote a book about his experiences in Antarctica, he mentioned a Fourth Presence that had once saved his life.

The story began in 1914 when Shackleton embarked on an ambitious plan to cross Antarctica by way of the South Pole. The expedition, the second he had made to the frozen continent, was jinxed from the start. He had hoped that the Weddell Sea off the coast of Antarctica would be navigable. Instead, unseasonable weather had broken up the firm sheet of ice that usually, at that time of year, lined the coast. Instead, smaller sheets of ice (called ice floes) of all shapes and sizes, along with icebergs, filled the bay. They crashed and ground against each other as storms roiled the waters below. Shackleton's ship was imprisoned in this churning jumble of ice blocks, and then it was crushed. On November 21, it sank, leaving the 28-man crew to survive as best it could.

It was the following April before there was sufficient open water to launch the three small boats the men had brought with them from their sinking ship. On these boats they made their way to isolated Elephant Island, which provided shelter, but little else. There was no chance of rescue from the island because ships bypassed it.

Shackleton decided to make his way to the island of South Georgia, where there was a large whaling station. Two of the three boats were too small to make the more than 800-mile journey there. Shackleton chose six men to accompany him in the largest boat. It took 16 days for them to reach King Haakon Bay on South Georgia. Enclosed by tall, rugged cliffs, the harbor was almost as isolated as Elephant Island. The men would have to get to the opposite side of South Georgia, where the whaling station was located.

The boat in which they had come was so battered by storms

and high seas that Shackleton was afraid it would never make the trip. Land passage was the only way, even though he knew the interior of the island was a gigantic death trap. No one had ever been able to cross it before.

Shackleton chose two able men, Worsley and Crean, to accompany him. They planned to travel light, taking only three days' rations, a primus lamp filled with oil, a small cooker, a few matches, an adze that could be used as an ice axe, and a 50-foot long alpine rope. Though it was bitter cold, they left their sleeping bags behind, because the weight would have slowed them down.

The trio set out at three o'clock in the morning. The sky was clear with a full moon shining. By its light the men threaded a path around the glacier that spilled down the cliffs

into Haakon Bay. It took them two hours to climb 2500 feet. From there they could look out on a mass of high peaks fronted by perpendicular cliffs. Steep snow slopes fell away in all directions. The frozen rivers of ancient glaciers glimmered in the moonlight.

Swallowing their fear, the men set off through the forbidding, frigid world. As they tramped through soft snow

Shackleton suddenly felt another presence, invisible but real, walking at his side. During the long, harrowing trek, the presence stayed with him. It was there when blinding fogs blanketed everything. The presence seemed to give him strength as, dangling from the rope, he chiseled steps in a glacier's steep slope for the men to follow. It built up his resolve when, time after time, he found himself going in the wrong direction and had to lead his men back along the hazardous way they had come. It was there, too, a protector and guide, as the three picked their way through mazes of dangerous crevasses, half-concealed by snow.

On the second night, exhausted, half-frozen, despairing, the men had to force themselves to trudge on under the cold moon. They didn't dare stop for sleep, because without their warm bags, sleep would end in death. Through the long hours, the presence continued to stay with them, lending courage and strength.

Finally, 36 hours after they had set out from King Haakon Bay, the men achieved the impossible. They reached the shore and the whaling station without any loss of life or serious injury. Never once had Shackleton mentioned the presence during the long trek. Perhaps he was afraid his men might think he had lost his mind. But to his amazement, Worsley broke the silence.

"Boss," he said, "you know, I had a curious feeling on the march there was another person with us." Quickly, Crean agreed. He had felt it too and been comforted and encouraged by it. But, like Shackleton, neither man had voiced his feelings aloud until that moment.

What could it have been that walked with Shackleton and his men during the hours they faced death in the lonely, tumbled wastes of a frozen island? Who was the Fourth Presence?

Lavender

In the fall of 1948, two students at the University of Chicago decided to escape the rigors of study in their stuffy dorm and attend a dance they had seen posted on the bulletin board. They had waited too long to find dates, but knew there would be many eager coeds at the festive affair.

While driving along the highway, they noticed a young girl slowly walking on the shoulder of the road. The boys stopped and invited the enchanting stranger to ride with them. She told them she was on her way to a dance and got into the car.

The boys introduced themselves and said they were also on their way to the dance. She smiled and said her name was the same as the lavender dress she was wearing. Although her beauty was alluring, there seemed to be something strange about their pretty passenger.

At the party, Lavender was an excellent dancer. All the boys surrendered to her beguiling charm and personality that evening. She captured the hearts of everyone except the other girls, who were virtually ignored by their dates.

When the dance hall closed, the two boys offered to take Lavender home. She smiled and slid onto the rear seat of the convertible. During the drive, the autumn air became chilly and one of the boys gave her his coat.

They were surprised when they arrived at her house. Lavender lived in a crumbling shack, standing precariously on a dirt road off the highway. They said good night and were soon on their way back to the campus.

During lunch the next day, the two students remembered that Lavender still had the coat. After class, they drove to the old shack on the outskirts of Chicago. They could not understand why such a wonderful girl had to live in such a grubby part of the city. An elderly woman answered their knock.

"Hello," said the older boy. "Is Lavender home?"

"Nobody named Lavender lives here," said the woman, who eyed the boys suspiciously. "What do you want?"

"She must live here," insisted the other boy. "We brought her home last night after a dance."

When he described her, the woman's face beamed with delight. "Oh, you must be talking about Lily. That's what she looked like. But Lily isn't here anymore." The old woman grinned shrewdly. "She lives in the cemetery down the road."

The two boys suddenly thought they were the victims of a practical joke and decided to let Lavender keep the jacket. She obviously did not own a coat or she would have worn it last night. Lavender could use some warm clothes if this hovel was really her home. They smiled, said good-bye to the old woman, and drove away in silence.

Out of curiosity, they went to the abandoned cemetery to check out the crazy story. Surely, the old woman was just having fun with them. As a matter of fact, she was probably still chuckling at their innocence.

At the cemetery, they began walking along the headstones and were mildly surprised to find a marker engraved with the name "Lily." But they were really shocked when they found their missing coat folded neatly on the grave.

INDEX

The Beautiful Blonde of Brentwood, 25–26

Bennett, Marsha, 6–7

The Boy with the Brass Buttons, 74–76

The Case of the Kitten Ghost, 32–34

Casino, Del, 29

Casino, Joe, 29

Colombo, Russ, 29

Davis, Dick, 46–47

Deadly Kindness, 64–66

Death at the Falls, 88–90

The Demonic Hairdresser, 51–52

The Doctor's Visit, 9–10

Dunn, Jack, 29–30

The Evil in Room 310, 6–7

Faces in the Sea, 59–60

The Fourth Presence, 91–93

Ghost Dog on the Stairway, 39–40

The Ghost of a Deformed Monk, 62

The Ghost of Dead Man's Curve, 11–12

The Ghost of Greylock, 46–47

Grey Lady of St. Thomas, 64–66

Hahn, Alfred, 30

The Haunted Cleaning Lady, 48–50

The Haunted Schoolhouse, 8

The Headless Lady, 44–45

A Horse Named Lady Wonder, 35–38

The Hunter and the Hunted, 80–82

Irving, Washington, 27

Jackson, Roy, 70–71

Johnson, Mary, 51–52

Kitten ghost, 32–34

Lady in White, 67–68

A Lady's Reign of Death, 67–68

Lady Wonder, 35–38

Larch, Oliver, 72–73

Lavender, 94–95

The Light in the Window, 13–14

Lucky at Cards, 16–17

Maeterlinck, Maurice, 62

The Man and the Glove, 83–84

Mitchell, Margaret, 24

Mitchell, Weir S., 9–10

Monroe, Marilyn, 25–26

Needham, Charles, 44–45

Negri, Pola, 28–29

Niagara Falls, 88–90

Not Gone with the Wind, 24

The Old Man of the Woods, 78–79

Perkins, Lucy, 8

The Phantom Stagecoach, 54–55

Pinkney, J. M., 56–58

Rowley, John, 20–22

The Runaway Locomotive, 56–58

Sam Plays the Ghost from South Troy, 18–19

Shackleton, Sir Ernest, 91–93

Sherbrooke, John, 63

Sherwood, Arthur, 20–21

Smith, Margo, 48–50

The Spell on the Mirror, 85–86

The Terrible Hand, 70–71

A Terrifying Visitor, 63

The Thing in the Cellar, 42–43

Valentino's Ring, 28–30

Van Paassen, Pierre, 39–40

Washington Irving Returns, 27

The Weekend Guest Who Wasn't There, 20–22

What Got Oliver Larch?, 72–73

Wynyard, George, 63